The Mindful Dragon
My Dragon Books – Volume 3
Written by Steve Herman

Copyright © 2018 by Digital Golden Solutions LLC.
Published by DG Books Publishing, an imprint of Digital Golden Solutions LLC.

Information contained within this book is for entertainment and educational purposes only. Although the author and publisher have made every effort to ensure that the information in this book was correct at press time, the author and publisher do not assume and hereby disclaim any liability to any party for any loss, damage, or disruption caused by errors or omissions, whether such errors or omissions result from negligence, accident, or any other cause.

ISBN: 978-1948040105 (paperback)
ISBN: 978-1948040204 (hardcover)

www.MyDragonBooks.com

First Edition: February 2018

10 9 8 7 6 5 4 3 2 1

The Mindful Dragon

My Dragon Books - Volume 3

Steve Herman

He won't breathe fire or roar at you,
even though he could --
Diggory Doo's a gentle pet,
for I've trained him to be good.

A dragon is not hard to train
for dragons are quite smart...

And underneath their dragon scales,
there beats a tender heart.

So not only must you train them to roll over, sit, and stay

But also to direct their thoughts to live a mindful way.

When I asked him what was wrong, he said, "I think my friends are mad."

I told him not to worry about what happened yesterday — "There's not a thing that you can do to change it, anyway!"

"If you want **TOMORROW** to turn out A-OK, You can't make it happen by worrying **TODAY**."

Just leave the *past* behind you
with its blunders and regret...

And don't fret about the *future*, for it's not happened yet.

Love your *PAST* for memories
and lessons that you've learned,
And there's no harm in planning
where your *FUTURE* is concerned.

Diggory Doo cocked his head
and wiped his tears away;
He listened very closely
to the things I had to say.

I told him it's called "*MINDFULNESS*" when you can clearly see That where you are this moment is where you're meant to be.

That's why we call **today** the **"present,"** for it is like a gift...

That we open with our senses
to give our hearts a lift.

Open up your eyes; do you see
Nature all around you?
Trees and flowers, birds and bees,
lakes and hills surround you?

Listen for the music when the wind blows through the pines...

Smell the fragrance of perfume
from the honeysuckle vines...

Taste the sweetness of the berry
when it bursts upon your tongue...

Dance barefoot through the dew
when the day is fresh and young.

Love the life you're blessed with,
as you embrace *Today*...

Your fears and your anxiety will surely melt away.

When you practice *mindfulness*, you have a lifetime plan.

And when you've mastered *mindfulness*,
don't keep it to yourself;
Don't put it in a box which
you store upon a shelf.

Read more about Drew and Diggory Doo!

POTTY TRAIN YOUR DRAGON
Steve Herman

TRAIN YOUR ANGRY DRAGON
Steve Herman

THE MINDFUL DRAGON
Steve Herman

THE YOGA DRAGON
Steve Herman

DRAGON & THE BULLY
Steve Herman

HAPPY BIRTHDAY DRAGON
Steve Herman

TRAIN YOUR DRAGON TO ACCEPT NO
Steve Herman

I GOT THIS!
Steve Herman

TRAIN YOUR DRAGON TO BE KIND
Steve Herman

A DRAGON With His Mouth ON FIRE
Steve Herman

TRAIN YOUR DRAGON To Follow RULES
Steve Herman

TRAIN YOUR DRAGON To Be RESPONSIBLE
Steve Herman

TRAIN YOUR DRAGON To LOVE HIMSELF
Steve Herman

TEACH YOUR DRAGON To Understand CONSEQUENCES
Steve Herman

TEACH YOUR DRAGON TO STOP LYING
Steve Herman

TEACH YOUR DRAGON TO MAKE FRIENDS
Steve Herman

Visit
www.MyDragonBooks.com
for more!

Made in the USA
Middletown, DE
15 February 2019